AQUILLO
COMICS

ISSUE #1

"EXPERIMENTS"

GRELL & TANDA

CREATED BY
DEION TILLETT

To order additional copies of this book, contact:
Xlibris
844-714-8691
www.Xlibris.com
Orders@Xlibris.com

ISBN: Softcover   978-1-6698-1888-5
        EBook   978-1-6698-1887-8

Print information available on the last page

Rev. date: 03/31/2022

ABANDONED UNDERGROUND FACILITY

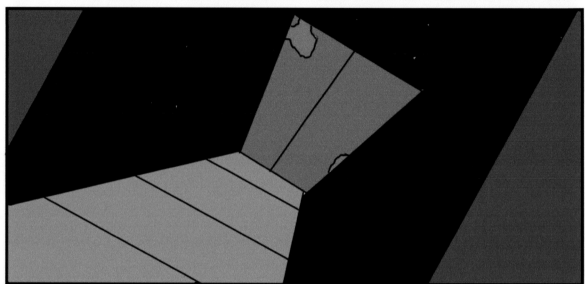

POD NUMBER 0045: ACTIVE

RELEASING CURRENT ASSET

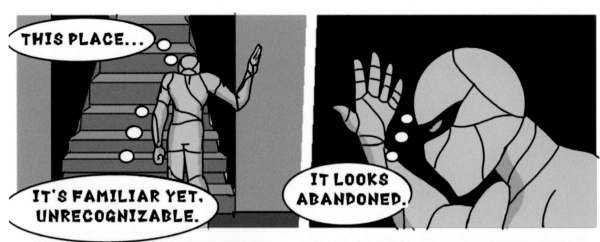

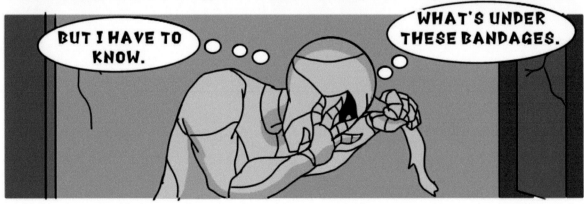

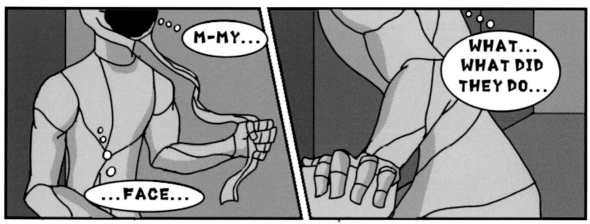

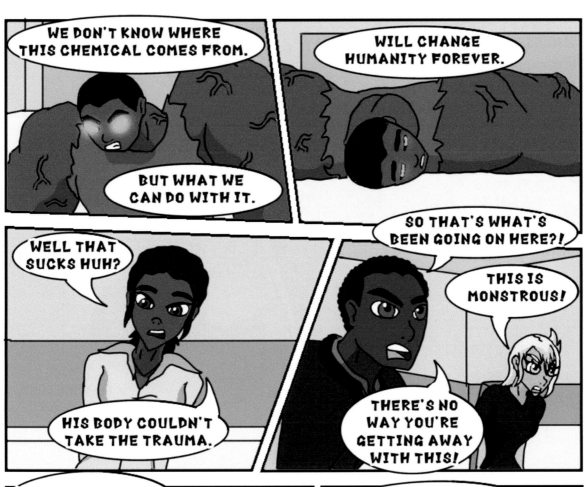

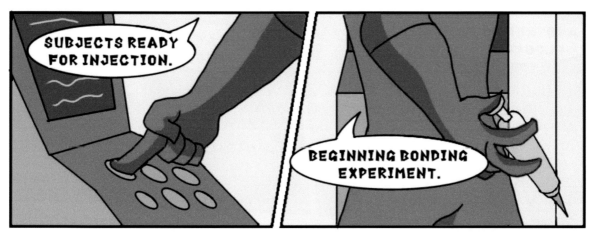

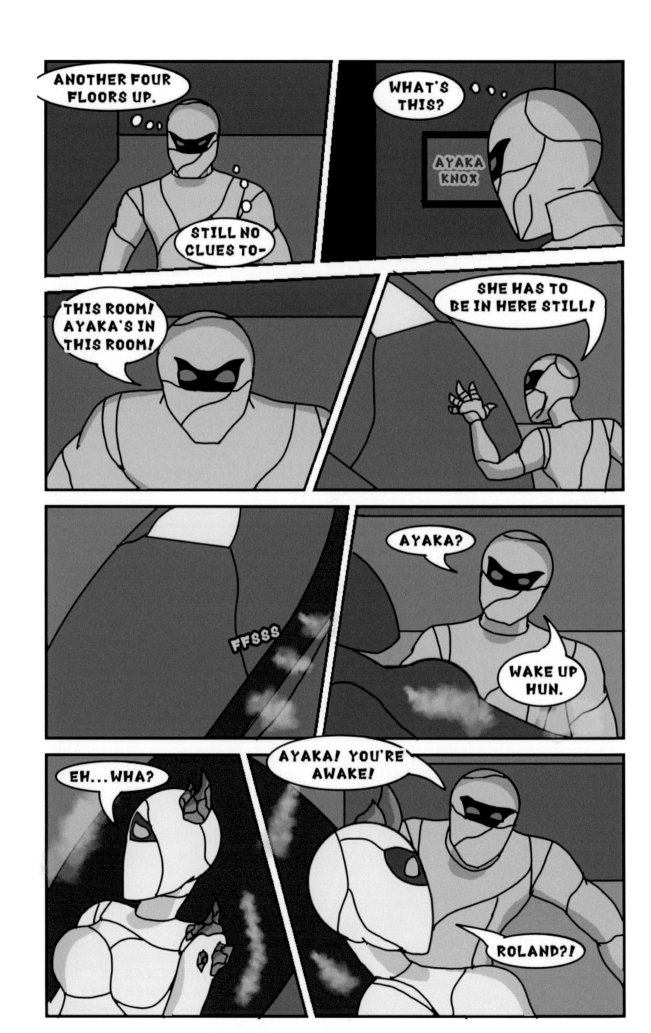

Printed in the United States
by Baker & Taylor Publisher Services